Renier-Fréduman Mundil

Allegories

Volume 4
Short Stories

Renier-Fréduman Mundil

Allegories

Volume 4
Short Stories

Translated from German
by Hilary Teske

Bibliographic information from the German National Library:
The German National Library lists this publication in the
German National Bibliography; detailed bibliographic data is
available online at http://dnb.dnb.de.

Cover design: Dan Winkler
Editing: Malin Friese
Publisher: BoD · Books on Demand GmbH,
Überseering 33, 22297 Hamburg, bod@bod.de
Print: Libri Plureos GmbH, Friedensallee 273,
22763 Hamburg

ISBN: 978-3-8192-9855-4

For
Celestine

Introduction

The allegory is a linguistic placeholder for the parable. To understand a person better, it is worth looking at their whole family. The family member parable has many relatives, obviously close relatives such as mother, father, brother and sister as well as those who have married in from some distant side, adopted, there are also first cousins (first degree) as well as untraceable 25th cousins (25th degree) and probably also a number of family members who are not such – those who simply went to the wedding party, although they had no connection to the family, but pretended to be a deeply connected family member.

A colourful mixture of kinship called allegory, analogy, comparison, simile, didactic piece, metaphor, allegory, similitude, maschal and nimschal and others.

As this picture is very colourful, we can easily imagine that parables not only play a role in the Jewish or Christian religion, but also in many other religions, cultures and poems.

The undisputed grandmaster of the parable is Jesus Christ. He is said to have told (sorry, I haven't counted) 48 parables in the New Testament.

The following is an extract:

- The fig tree (with and without fruit)
- Creditor and two debtors
- House built on rock and sand
- The guest without a wedding garment
- The wise and foolish virgins
- The pearl of great price
- The camel and the eye of the needle
- New wine in old wineskins
- The leavened bread
- The unmerciful creditor
- Treasure in the field
- Mustard seed
- Entrusted talents
- Tares and wheat
- The Last Judgement
- The unjust judge
- The prodigal son
- The lost sheep
- The lost coin
- The Good Samaritan
- The sower

Although Christ used everyday life at that time for his parables - for example, there were no street lamps, everyone walked with an oil lamp, the seed was not sown with millimetre precision using a machine but was scattered by hand, seeds fell on stones, under weeds, etc. – although he used these situations, which we rarely encounter in our everyday lives, they still leave a deep impression today. They are easy to remember with a hidden important message that we discover when we think about them.

One of the things that impressed me was the parable of the five wise and five foolish virgins. All ten waited for the Lord, who did not come at the expected time. When he appeared, the oil lamps were empty. The five wise virgins had a reserve, refilled their lamps and were invited to the wedding feast in heaven. The five foolish ones first had to go to the city to refill their lamps. When they stood at the gates of heaven, these were and remained closed. They were too late, a moment too late because of their negligence, and this brief moment meant that they had to stand outside the locked gates of heaven for an eternity.

This parable reminded me of an incident with my father. We were repairing the drain in the kitchen at home and realised just before we finished that a piece was missing. So we rushed off, ran to the underground, travelled seven stops and rushed to the nearest plumbing shop. Back then, there were no large, almost permanently open DIY shops, and there was no such thing as same-day express delivery via the internet. None of that existed yet.

We arrived at the small shop at exactly 1.01 pm, 1 minute after closing time. Behind the glass pane, we saw the owner locking the door at various levels. We were able to talk to him through the glass door, complaining about our misery, a weekend without normal drainage of the dishwater, no, we would have to dispose of each bowl separately. None of it helped. The owner would not budge. We were standing in front of a closed toilet cubicle for a minute.

That day, there wasn't another young person in the world who understood the five foolish virgins better than I did.

Parables come to life when we look at them through our everyday lives, even if they look different (but only outwardly) from the time of Christ.

The German word Geglichenes (here translated as allegory) also has relatives: Ausgeglichenes (balance), Abgeglichenes (alignment), Beglichenes (settlement), Verglichenes (comparison) and certainly even more relatives. If we join each of these different family members and look at the parable from the different positions, then a rounded picture emerges from everything, which is what we often strive for in life.

In every parable there is an equation made up of a number of unknowns.

      1. OT + NT = BB or

      2. OT + NT = L

The first equation is simple:

OT (Old Testament) + **NT** (New Testament) = **BiBle**.

But the second equation has another explanation. OT is not only the **Old Testament** but also **Ordinary Times**.

O(rdinary)**T**(imes) + **N**(ew) **T**(estament) = Life.

That is the equation behind the parables: the ordinary times links up with the New Testament or the parables so abundant there and results in

(=) life. And which of us doesn't like to understand our complicated lives through this simple equation?

The following collection contains just over 60 short stories, each of which is based on a biblical passage, usually from the New Testament. As we have four children, the stories are deliberately divided into four volumes, a small legacy to the children to discover in their own lives or the lives of their own families the precious treasure of the parables that Christ so often used. A short time to catch your breath, a short time perhaps to reflect, a short time perhaps to delve deeper.

1.
Groundbreaking or Working Faith

The word had spread everywhere. The country was filled with the news. Without television, telephone, cell phone, newspaper, internet, courier service, it had spread a thousand times faster: the incredible news of his miracles. There was nothing he couldn't do. Reading someone else's mind. Recognizing the pitfalls of the law in good time. Maneuvering between the various powers without becoming vulnerable. He was the bright ray of sunshine for children, the hero of youth, the hope of women in their oppressed position, the light on the horizon for the poor, the needy, the desperate, the terminally ill, the possessed, the weary, the lame, the blind, the lepers, beggars, thieves, prostitutes, tax collectors.

And now he had come to their village. Sitting in a small house, people hanging in the windows so that at least one of his glances would catch them, an uncountable crowd gathered around the house, shouting, tugging, everyone fighting to get a few centimeters closer to him.

Nathan lay on his bed. For many years. Paralyzed in the legs, only a few of his arm muscles still animated with some strength. There was a knock. Before he answered, the door opened. His brother and his friend entered, his father and one of his uncles were waiting outside.

We'll take you to him, Eli said.

To whom? Nathan's voice was weak.

To the Lord. He has come to our village. A great miracle for us.

He won't allow me to see him. We have no money.

The Lord does not take money. It is an advantage that you are poor. The first time in your life that poverty is an advantage.

What should I tell him?

Nothing, he knows why we're bringing you.

He will ask about my faith. I've been lying on this bed too long to have faith.

He will see our faith and it will be enough for him.

You need your faith for yourselves. Don't you have any requests for him?

Yes, but your request comes first. It is greater.

The years had made him bitter, suspicious. Was it not selfishness on the part of the others, they no longer had to worry about him once he was healthy. On the contrary. He was in their debt. The many years of their help. They would expect him to repay them to the best of his ability.

He was lost in bitter thoughts when they dragged him out into the daylight. The sun was blinding, he hid his face under the blanket. Outside, people were shouting, their venomous looks could be felt through the woolen blanket as they had to leave because of him. But his friends were undeterred, spreading the crowd like a plow ripping up the earth.

There was nowhere to go in front of the house. It was impossible to get in. No-one was prepared to give way any further, no-one who was in the house would voluntarily come out to make way for him.

Eli, his friend, jumped onto a man's shoulder and from there on to the roof of the house. It was lightning fast. Before the crowd knew it, the first bricks fell to the ground. Seized by terror, the people scattered. The friends carried the stretcher through the cleared passageway and Eli kept tearing the tiles off the roof. Then they lifted him up and carefully lowered him into the house, right in front of the Lord's feet.

The Lord did not look up, he had long since seen everything.

It became deathly quiet. No-one dared to breathe. Even the teachers of the law, who were busy arguing, were silent.

Jesus thought about the faith that the people had shown. And the Lord said to him:

Your sins are forgiven. (Luke 5:20)

And he knew that the Lord could not lie.

2.

2.

Late Turnaround

His appearance in the pulpit outshone everyone and everything, even the Lord hanging on the cross above the altar. Everything was just an accessory, an adornment, for his powerful words. For today, he had prepared the crown of his sermons, a symphony of praise for the archbishop and minor-key announcements of punishment for wretched sinners, a masterpiece of words, interrupted in the right places by booming chords from the organ to give the audience a taste of purgatory. Every little detail had been rehearsed, the entries had been practiced many times with the organist, at the climax of the judgment the choir's performance, Dies irae, from Verdi's Requiem, made even him shudder every time.

Then the color of the words would change, sweet sounds of the psalms would flow through the old church, behind them increasing praises of the Lord and at the end the power of the word and the music united, Handel's Hallelujah, at the end of which he would call out with a sonorous voice: Amen and Amen and Amen.

He could not come up with the Lord's miracles, so the effect of the word, the power of the music, had to compensate and his stately appearance had to impress the eyes of the listeners. But it was not enough, how was his tall, powerful, stately appearance supposed to fit into this structure in a dignified manner, to capture the archbishop's attention a little more and keep the audience at an appropriate distance when his body was in the gown he wore year in, year out.

Only because his housekeeper had so irreparably mangled the newly made robe that it was no longer even suitable for the rag collection. The flat iron had burnt a huge hole in it where the fabric lay against the left breast, the heart. Why on earth didn't she let the phone ring and finish ironing first? He could get sick. No, there was no alternative, he longed for the bath in the power of his words, only with the right swimming suit it was over.

So, he would put on the old suit. The force of his words would cover up this flaw. Snorting with rage, he stomped the short distance from the vicarage to the old church.

His steps quickened of their own accord, drawn by the pull of the crowd waiting for him. If only he could have taken up his position in the pulpit before everyone else, his worn robe hidden behind the parapet, his radiant, shining face turned towards the expectant listeners. His steps quickened further, faster, he left the balmy summer wind behind him and dashed across the courtyard.

The words of his sermon raced through his head. His hand rose, admonishing, weighty, holding the audience in thrall like a conductor taming the orchestra. The powerful chords of the organ roared from within, the thick old walls of the church began to vibrate with the force of the sounds, he heard the gnashing teeth of repentant sinners, felt the storm of purgatory roaring ominously through the open door of the house of God.

He had told the old housekeeper to stay at home. The sight of her would infuriate him, sure, it was Sunday, but the Lord had not known about housekeepers when he had walked the earth, only spoken of duty. Why shouldn't the old woman do her duty on Sunday?

Suddenly it became quiet. The organ had fallen silent, the breathing of those waiting had died away, the balmy summer wind rested in the green treetops, a single bird let its song resound through the mild Sunday morning. He stopped, he didn't want to, but he resigned himself to the suspended moment of time. The bird's bright chimes floated through the air and turned into soft words in the balmy summer breeze, whispering across the courtyard.

Therefore, if you are offering your gift at the altar and there remember that your brother or sister has something against you, leave your gift there in front of the altar. First go and be reconciled to them; then come and offer your gift. (Matthew 5:23-25).

His feet turned and he followed the trail of the spoken melody that carried his steps back to the rectory, while in the massive church the minor-keyed organ roared anew, its heavy music pounding down on those waiting helplessly at the empty pulpit.

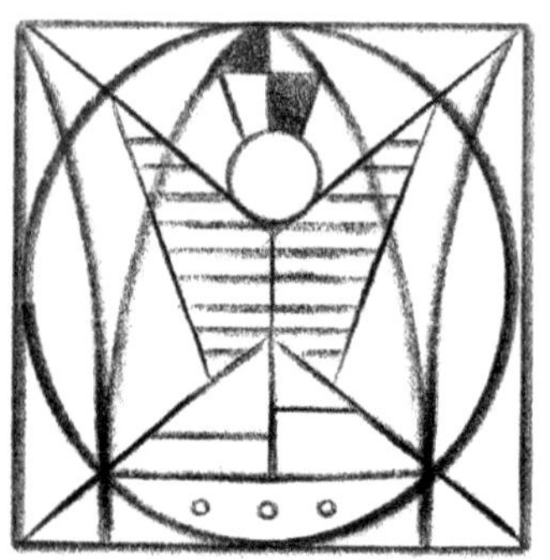

3.
Fisher Of Men

The catch was meagre, less than a quarter of what they were used to, not even a tenth of what they had hoped for. They had been working on the new net for months, countless knots soaked in their blood as they squatted in front of the hut in the evening, exhausted from the long boat trip to catch fish, to finish the new fishing gear, guiding their needles unsteadily and hitting their own fingers instead of the opening of the traps. The old net was tattered, only a week ago it was full to bursting, what a sight, the thousands of silver fish, when it tore open full to bursting on the rough wooden side of the boat and the fat catch disappeared into the expanse of the lake. Their hope and confidence drove them on. The new one would be better, everything new would be better, the work would be easier, the catch would be bigger, they would be able to shorten their working hours, go out an hour later, no more setting off into the unknown in the cold fog.

James, John, make haste.

Their father Zebedee's voice sounded tense, strained, tired, irritated.

Have I not taught you to understand the sky? The clouds, look. A storm will break out in a few hours.

The two sons were silent, no answer, but their fingers now darted like busy ants between the meshes of the new net.

In front of them lay their lives, their livelihood, everything depended on this net, food that had to be bought, materials to repair the small fishing hut, the taxes before the fierce soldiers arrived to collect them by force, the price for the animals, offerings in the temple to please the Lord, and, and, and.

And suddenly he stood before them. This itinerant preacher Jesus, his miracles were spreading faster than wildfire through the land. His shadow fell on the net so that the meshes melted into a dark black surface before their eyes. He stood calmly before them, his eyes seeming to examine all the knots of the net as if to count the drops of blood they had shed in their work.

No greeting, no question about their well-being, as if out of nowhere his figure had appeared, interposing itself between them and the sun. The next moment, his mouth opened:

Come here, follow me. I will make you fishers of men. (Matthew 4:19)

He saw the two brothers jump up. It had been the same with Peter and Andrew. They jumped out of the boat, leaving the new, almost finished net behind them like the boat, their father Zebedee, their mother, who was now cooking in the little hut and would heap lamentations on her husband in the evening because of the departure of her two sons, did not return to the hut again, They left their little brothers and sisters behind, shedding tears at not having their strong older brothers around them, and jumped out of the boat straight into their new life.

Less than five minutes later, they had disappeared from her father's sight, and he was still watching the scene with his mouth agape but unable to understand.

He had read this story more than a hundred times, heard it, been told it, taken it apart, tried to elicit the last secrets from the few words. Countless times, but only today, this one time, he felt the stab in his heart. His life was gasping for air, all his thoughts were spinning in a jumble in his head. He couldn't grasp any of them, dizziness seized him before he sank to the ground, his eyes went black, the stabs in his heart and the blackness in front of his eyes merged into a strange formation. Black spots dissolved, leaving behind rough dark lines, the strange structure had turned into a huge net in which he was trapped. He searched for an exit, in vain, he tried to tear the gaiters, in vain, tried to bite through the ropes with his teeth, in vain, he was trapped in a huge net.

What do you fish people with? he thought.

Fishers of men, an unreal word. Where were the humans swimming? Which ones could he catch, which ones did he have to throw back into the sea, which sea in general, how big could the meshes be so that no-one could slip through? He had better bait them. Not so many could be caught, but special specimens, more valuable ones, what nonsense ran through him, could there be more valuable ones when fishing for people? Why not? What if a predatory fish, a shark, was attached to the bait he had cast out?

Slowly the thoughts became less. Slowly the net dissolved. James and John had disappeared, as had the abandoned Zebedee in his boat, the figure of the Lord, the tears of his mother and little brothers and sisters – everything had vanished.

When he looked up, he saw the face of the dark-skinned child on the poster. He could see the boy, but the boy could not see him. Not because he was on the poster, not because he was not a reality in his room, not because it was from another time. The boy was blind. The child's eyes stared at him. Fixed him, pierced his gaze, his eyes, his head, and disappeared from his room through the open door. Only the lifeless shell of the child was left behind. Africa, lions, zebras, monkeys, thousands of wondrous flowers, exotic-looking fruit, a paradise.

The boy lived in a paradise, but didn't realize it. The lifeless eyes of the boy staring down at him from the poster were expressionless.

Help, he read under the picture. Just €70 and the child can see again.

The lion, the monkey, the crocodile, the boy would see them all. €70 was the cost of a tiny operation to restore the child's sight. He had heard about this strange disease. But he didn't like fundraising campaigns like this. How much money was squandered in the administration, fraudsters were probably pocketing some of it for themselves, corrupt doctors were charging more for the operation, countless sensible, comprehensible arguments against donating were neatly laid out on the page of his analytical mind.

His feet started moving of their own accord. Before he knew it, he had dressed and was suddenly standing at the counter of his bank. He had known the woman for many years. Talked about her as his personal advisor. He had discussed investment strategies with her and, over time, through consistent saving and a few smart decisions, had managed to amass a small fortune of €50,000 with her. For his trip around the world. A sabbatical. To travel for a year. America, Canada, Asia, Australia, New Zealand and Africa. Last but not least, Africa. He jerked at the word Africa.

The employee looked at him in bewilderment.

Do you know exactly what you're doing?
He nodded wordlessly.

Sleep on it one more night, she advised him.

He shook his head.

Should I find out about some hedge funds? the woman asked.

He shook his head again.

Maybe half, the woman said. Donate half, that's still more than most people do.

He shook his head.

And the other children, he muttered. The net is big enough for all the children.

The woman became suspicious. Maybe he was confused, sick, didn't know what he was doing. She turned to fetch the bank manager.

Please don't, he said, as if he could read her mind.

During the brief conversation, he had entered the amount on the check and signed it. He had jumped into a new life. He would only realize later what he had left behind. A strange time, he thought.

What do you fish people with? With money. Maybe, maybe not.

Fishing for people, he muttered, it had become clear to him that you could only become a fisher of men if you weren't on the bait hook of money yourself.

That much was certain. How else would someone else be able to bite if you were on the hook yourself?

The customer was informed in detail about the extent of his action. It was a small sentence that the advisor entered into the documents for his own protection as he was leaving the bank. He felt a small jolt, just a tiny nip, a brief up and down. He turned around slightly, the woman was wearing a silver dress made of thousands of scales, her eyes staring at the check. The hook danced in the water, incessantly up and down, on the verge of disappearing into the depths. He had known her for many years and knew immediately what this meant.

4.

Pecuniary Non-theory Of Relativity

She leafed through the glossy pages of the brochure. Fine beads of sweat from her excitement spread across the smooth surface. Her fingers felt the paper. With a little imagination, she felt the huge, straw-like mane of the giant predatory cat.

A lion, what a wonderful animal. Calm, majesty and grandeur shone into her eyes from every angle. Her pupils fevered through the small black letters. 100 %. 100% guarantee. Unbelievable, but she believed it. It was 100% guaranteed that every traveler on the safari would see at least one lion, no, not just one, she read on, a whole pride of lions. Likewise with the giraffes, zebras anyway, pumas, leopards.

Everything guaranteed 100%.

She hastily jumped up, rushed to the cupboard and fetched the expensive SLR digital camera. She aimed the lens and pressed the shutter. Trapped on the tiny photo chip, the large animal figure rose up and started to jump, its front paws leaving the ground. Startled, her fingers opened, and the expensive camera was catapulted to the ground. Anticipation played tricks with the old woman's mind.

The wrinkled hands slid to the floor, snatched the camera from gravity and pressed the small display into her left eye. She breathed a sigh of relief. The lion was still clearly visible. The warranty insured by the high price had not let her down. The expensive camera worked as if it could hardly wait to capture the animals of the savannah with its lens.

Few of its camera sisters and brothers were granted the opportunity to see the animals of the savannah in the flesh in Africa. The camera recognized its purpose and would do anything to accompany the old woman on safari.

Suddenly it became moist.

The old woman's lips had planted a kiss on it. Barely recovered, it was then that he noticed another liquid, a stream of salty tears poured over it. No matter, it had been designed to endure everything. Heat, cold, rain, even human emotional outbursts. Shortly afterwards, it became dark around it, scarlet silk enveloping its black body as the woman's still shaking hands pushed it back into the precious leather bag.

Ever since she was a little girl, she had dreamed of meeting the wild animals of Africa on a safari. Many times at the zoo, countless animal shows on television, meters of illustrated books. Everything was a world away from an encounter in the wild.

Life had not meant well. As a sales clerk, she had fought a duel with life, her husband had vanished far too early into that unfathomable heaven above her, only a few short vacations, a rare concert visit, going out to eat was unthinkable, almost every non-essential penny disappeared into the piggy bank, so excellently hidden in the small apartment that she sometimes couldn't find it herself straight away.

Now the sum had been climbed like a Mount Everest peak and tomorrow, she pinched herself, it was a reality, tomorrow, really tomorrow she would visit the travel agency. A little exhausted from the excitement, she fell into the greasy, worn armchair.

In front of her, as if by magic - yes, didn't everyone have a magic hand these days - a small click captured the wide world on the screen, and a black pane of glass began to transform into images in front of her.

She wasn't looking for anything special, just a bit of switching, watching, listening, then switching off, going to bed early and straight to the traveler's office in the morning.

She skipped the commercials, not always, but often enough to avoid the temptation to spend money and jeopardize the safari. Her slightly unworldly conviction held firm: lions, tigers and giraffes were just waiting to be eyed by her.

When she looked up, she saw the small, dark-skinned child. It lay motionless in the arms of a woman, staring directly into her pupils from eerily huge eyes. Like cuts from a Japanese filleting knife, they cut through her other senses, only snatches of words penetrated her head: 800 million, hunger, suffering, death, 800 million, aid, Africa, South America.

Intuitively she reached for a scrap of paper, it was useless, nowhere could she see a partnering pen. So she took the plate on which two buttered pieces of bread lay and scribbled the numbers with her fingernails, which now appeared under the staring gaze of the swollen child.

A minute later, the spook was gone. A nightmare, she tried to reassure herself, she hadn't just been leafing through glossy Africa.

Just a bad nightmare.

The butter on her index finger destroyed the dream of the nightmare. More than obvious, everything was reality, thousands of kilometers away, as if by magic, by her magic hand, brought into the reality of her own life. She got up in silence. She found the piggy bank immediately, as if it had conspired with the television and was just waiting for her to appear.

She marveled in disbelief at the calmness of her hands as she counted the money. A second time to be on the safe side. As if it were yesterday, she remembered the important days over 50 years ago, when she once went hungry, really hungry, unintentionally, the cutting pain in her stomach, crazy thoughts, her fingers scraping the hardened crumbs from the corners of the bread box and pushing them into her parched mouth, the attempt to escape to sleep, to escape the terrible pain and thoughts for a few hours, everything close, tangible, as if she were right in the middle of it.

She took a small sheet of paper from the drawer, it was a bank transfer form, wrote the amount she had counted in the gray highlighted boxes, with the account number scratched in butter above it. Now she had to go to bed, she had to leave the apartment early, to the sterile glass box in which the money flowed.

The way led past the travel agency, she knew it, realized it, even in the mounting fatigue of the battle she had unconsciously waged against herself inside, she knew it, she knew everything, not everything, but everything that was important and that was certainly not important.

This poor widow has put in more than all the others. All these people gave their gifts out of their wealth; but she out of her poverty put in all she had to live on. (Luke 21:3,4)

Also, more than a few billionaires in this bleak world who, in a fit of kindness, gave 10% of their fortune as boomerang charity, hoping for a place next to the widow in the still distant unfathomable heaven above everyone's heads.

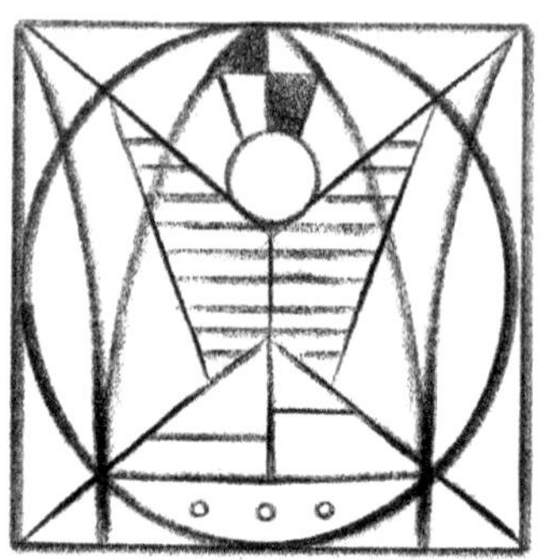

5.

High Times Before The Low

Where had he not seen it all? Not everything was what was commonly referred to as the most important event in life, at least in the past, and in quite a few parts of this rotating dirt ball earth.

The wedding. Marriage. Total amore. Center, one single center in the miniature cosmos of one's own limited world. For a mathematician, this observation would lead to the logical consequence of drawing a line under it. The wedding was the most important thing. Right. The wedding was the highlight of life. Right. Right and the end. It was all downhill after that. Mathematical consequence: the final line after this event. Was geometry used to place the location of the line to the exact millimeter on lifelines? Then the final line after the wedding night. This is part of the wedding anyway, even if the bride and groom had long since said their goodbyes, the guests on the officially ordered dance floor were drumming, dancing, staggering, continued merrily, so that mathematically speaking, the wedding party continued. The end was exactly after the wedding, on the wedding night lifeline.

What a prospect: no downhill slide, no future stress with parents-in-law, no stress when looking for an apartment later on, no stress with rebellious children, no stress with wedding days, no stress ... none, none, none anywhere.

Closing line climax – none, what a triad. A little, precisely calculated, by the gram. Did he shudder at the thought? His thoughts contributed to undermining the unique peak position of this event. Others dug with less, usually more diligently.

Enough, there were enough closing lines, so here was another one. Putting an end to the idea of at least being a dictator and ruler over one's own thoughts. Not bad. Not everyone could claim to be in this position – even outside of psychiatry.

He was startled. Now it was finally over; his thoughts had started at the wedding and ended up in the conceptual world of psychiatry. Three final lines. He ordered his head to draw three lines, to get his rebellious thoughts under control.

Images flashed up. Over time, weddings had been celebrated in almost every place on this rotating ball of dirt. As a diver in the depths of the sea. Crashing as a parachutist in the air. On a mountain peak. Even on Mount Everest? He didn't know. On a mountain peak for sure. Mount Everest? Here the Internet had to be contacted. A little later, he smiled with Viennese relaxation, a little later. On a dung heap? Another question mark, contact the Internet – wedding dung heap, later, a little later.

Only recently during a normal flight. All the important people in her life – mother, grandmother, siblings – sprang up like mushrooms from the floor below the rows of seats in front of the unsuspecting bride in her everyday clothes. She had not noticed them boarding. For safety's sake, they had been placed behind the bride on the plane. Her friend stood up and suddenly knelt down in front of her. Her mother approached her, a wedding dress in her arms. Other unsuspecting passengers pulled out tons of cell phones. A flood of pictures poured out of the plane on to the Internet. One picture could have been asked to look for a wedding on a dung heap in the labyrinth of the Internet as it flew by. In the meantime, she had put on her wedding dress and the pilot was standing in front of her.

Who was actually flying the plane now?

Never mind, there were more important things. After the second yes, there was thunderous applause, and behind the cloud of applause, the groom pressed a kiss to his wife's mouth, which was once again speechless. As the groom, he had been the owner of a woman's mouth for a few moments, so it mattered little whether she continued to revolt against his strange mouth.

Final line. Kiss on it. Together what belongs together. He had topped them all. In reality? In the world of thoughts? It didn't matter. What idiocy to draw distinctions between thoughts and reality. Money didn't matter. If it was not possessed, the mathematically logical consequence: it was imagined. Since the brain was no longer allowed to differentiate between thoughts and reality, it was obliged to release the same amount of happiness hormone for every millionth gram of imagined money. That was what mattered, the millionth gram of happiness hormone.

The gleaming white dress rose against the backdrop of the bubbling masses of lava. Fine, sulfurous vapors rose up. Like a brass band, noise-filled vapors were released from time to time into the vibrating air. Everything seemed to be a peaceful atmosphere. Above the fiery spectacle lay a carpet of deep blue air, the bride's swooping eyes competed with the sky and the most beautiful blue.

The wedding ceremony was kept brief. After the obligatory exchange of rings and – to equalize the antigen structures – the subsequent kiss to exchange lip surface antigen secretions, the music started with thumping basses and, in the true meaning of the word, the dance on the volcano began.

A group of young men armed themselves with spears, shortly afterwards massive T-bone steaks adorned their steel spears, and they ran several meters closer to the crater rim. Soon the lumps of meat, which a few days ago were still grazing on meadows dressed in fur, were sizzling in the hot, rising volcanic air. Melting, dripping fat emitted hissing sounds that combined with the sounds of the volcanic bubbling and the pounding bass to form a formidable orchestra.

The groom let his eyes wander briefly over his friends, most of his thoughts of alcohol had already rushed ahead to the wedding night, while the rest of him enjoyed imagining the source of images of this first volcanic wedding that would soon be flooding the Internet. Even the countless sparks of ash that had settled on the bride's white wedding dress and left behind fine clumps of fabric did not detract from this.

The sum of his thoughts did not reach any further, did not reach into the blue sky, did not reach beyond it into the universe, did not reach beyond it into the center of this unimaginable something – where He had long since decided to draw the line to the exclusion of all other beings.

Just as it was in the days of Noah, so also will it be in the days of the Son of Man. People were eating, drinking, marrying and being given in marriage up to the day Noah entered the ark. Then the flood came and destroyed them all.

It was the same in the days of Lot. People were eating and drinking, buying and selling, planting and building.

But the day Lot left Sodom, fire and sulfur rained down from heaven and destroyed them all. It will be just like this on the day the Son of Man is revealed. (Luke 17:26-30)

A flood was a flood, whether it was a flood of water or a flood of fire, did it make any difference?

6.

The Unknown Double Mark

He rushed through the polished aisles of the supermarket: chocolate spread, muesli, sliced cheese, slices of sausage cut out of an animal, toothpaste together with toilet paper, everything disappeared into the shopping cart, which stretched out its open crocodile mouth towards him. After feeding the lower half, he pressed a button on the handlebar, the subtotal lit up on the display, followed shortly afterwards by a special offer from the meat department.

Suddenly he felt something sticky on his finger. How could it be, he had obviously cut himself. He looked at the viscous red mass oozing from the skin of his finger. He shook his head in disbelief. Impossible. It was unbelievable. He hadn't cut himself. When the special offer from the meat department flashed up – a juicy steak – animal blood had been squeezed on to his finger from a pore in the trolley handle – reinforcing the advertising, so to speak.

Disgust welled up.

What went too far... went too far, Mount Everest-style. Bottomless impudence. But not bottomless. The impudence would have disappeared again. They wouldn't get away with it that easily.

Excuse me, may I help you.
Turning round, he recognized a young woman. Her uniform revealed her to be an employee of the supermarket, her dress super tight and short for advertising or other reasons. His anger disappeared faster than he could register it.

Not blood, said the pretty young woman. We won't go that far. (Not yet, her thoughts seemed to add). Ketchup, excellent, organic of course and 100% matched to the steak. You were just going to buy that, weren't you?
Before he could produce an answer, her hands had pleasantly embraced and cleaned his ketchup finger.
The only thing missing was the kiss, he thought. Her mouth enveloped his finger, and a pleasant warmth rose up inside him. His thoughts went crazy for a moment. But unfortunately, it was only the damp tissue paper, he realized disappointedly in the end.

Before he could wait to see what thoughts would run through his brain next, hopefully touching the limbic system, he held a cool packet in his hand. It was the steak, as a promotional sequence he was about to pick up the piece of meat from the meat counter.

Red, bloody, watery liquid swirled between the perfectly marbled lump of meat and the tight plastic packaging. It felt a little creepy, this woman, this supermarket, perhaps an analytical computer, someone, something seemed to know 100% of his taste.

He was hardly surprised that the woman had meanwhile pressed a bottle of organic ketchup into his other hand.

We recommend this new seasoning, the perfect harmonious combination between the steak, the ketchup and...

Suddenly he had the feeling that his wife was standing next to him, trying to convince him of her choice of next vacation destination and...

The woman bit her lips:

Excuse me, of course, also the perfect seasoning for the potatoes, I must have forgotten to bring it to you already.

Before he could say anything in reply, she had disappeared into the next aisle, only to return immediately afterwards with a net of small, firm potatoes and some deep green broccoli.

He felt even creepier. Broccoli, the only vegetable his taste buds were allowed to overrun, he had picked up a piece almost every time he went shopping. But not in this supermarket, he thought, he bought the vegetables from the health food store across the road on organic and other principles.

We're all connected, the young woman whispered.

She looked nervously behind her. Obviously, she should never have made that remark. She had made a dangerous faux pas.

Don't worry, he whispered back. I'm good at keeping quiet.

He would have liked to continue talking to her. But she put potatoes and broccoli in his shopping cart and put on a fleeting smile. Two small children and a grumpy husband were probably waiting for her at home, he consoled himself. Her shapely, barely clothed body had disappeared, only the meaningless shadow crawled across the polished floor and finally disappeared into the next aisle.

He didn't notice that the shopping cart was now rolling through the departments as if of its own accord, dragging him along like the trailer of a locomotive. The display lit up twice more, but the pores of the handle on the shopping cart remained closed. The young woman did not reappear either. He reached the checkout, which was free of cashiers, and placed the bulging shopping cart on the short conveyor belt. It guaranteed a slow, steady feed so that the control scanner could capture every item. After the scanner had compared its result with the number on the display on the shopping cart and found a 100 percent match, an automatic arm moved forward from the side and dropped a wrapped gift into his cart as a thank you for his honesty.

Now the machine arm moved from the horizontal to the vertical position and briefly asked:

Head or hand?

Head or hand, he repeated quietly.

He was glad to belong to the head faction. Previously unthinkable, until a few courageous pioneers had literally got their way – only a tiny scar on his forehead was a reminder of the decision made several years ago.

Previously, the bank account chip could only be implanted in the hand. Soon, however, the first people insisted on having it implanted under the skin of the forehead. This allowed the customer to keep both hands free. With his head through the wall, out of the wall of the supermarket, he thought mockingly as he stretched his forehead towards the raised automatic arm. The arm lowered, for a fraction of a second, only noticeable to the subconscious, it remained in a strictly upward-facing position, only to disappear more quickly, almost guilty, into oblivion.

By the time he pushed the shopping cart off the short conveyor belt, the data from his purchase had long since been swallowed up by a server lurking like a monster in a well-cooled chamber. And his result of a correct purchase was on the fiber optic path to a cloud-scratching glass-and-steel building that seemed to smile benevolently. Address: Sixth Street, number six, in the sixth neighborhood.

It also forced all people, great and small, rich and poor, free and slave, to have a mark on the right hand or forehead. Without the mark of the name of the Beast or the number of its name, it was impossible to buy or sell anything. Solve a riddle: Put your heads together and figure out the meaning of the number of the Beast. The mark of the Beast is a physical or spiritual mark that is required for people to buy or sell anything. This mark is a sign of loyalty and worship to the Antichrist, and those who refuse to take the mark are unable to participate in economic activities. The mark is also connected to the name or number of the Beast, which is the number 666. (Revelation 13:16-18)

In the hallway of the exit, he passed an inconspicuous office door. Behind it, visible at most to his intuition, stood the pretty young woman in front of her boss. She held a piece of paper out to him, which evoked a satisfied smile with a hint of mockery.

Seventy, he murmured, seventy steaks, the cattle will resent it. We have to find out immediately whether the abattoir can deliver more at short notice.

Seventy, he murmured once more. Poor live cattle. But well, fortunately no veal knuckles. No veal knuckles, even I don't want to imagine how many extra little calves they would bring to their deaths. Your account, my dear, your account, I can promise you that much, your account will be more than happy over the seventy.

Well, to be or not to be. Sometimes being made him happy, sometimes not being. At the same time, he emitted primal sounds into the air, noisily leaving his wife, steaks, veal knuckles, being and non-being.

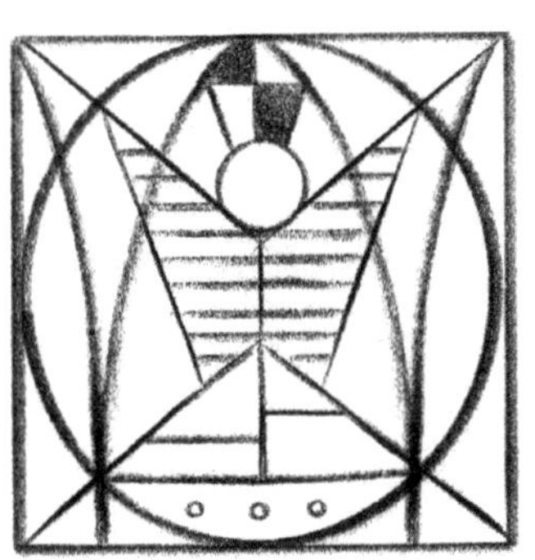

7.
Untalented Talent (?)

Five and five are ten. Josse placed five small sacks filled with grain next to five empty ones. Two and two are four, he mumbled, not ten, but still twice as much as at the beginning.

He looked at the old book. At some point the door will open and the Lord will enter, powerful like the prophet Elijah, for whose appearance they waited every year on one day, leaving the houses open.

His grandfather took it particularly seriously and not only put a place setting on the empty table, no, the best food on the table was placed on the prophet Elijah's plate. Only Elijah had never come before. And the food? Even if Elijah did come, would he eat at all? Would he, in his majesty as an immortal being, have to put up with the nothingness of food?

No matter, so far Elijah had never appeared in any year, the place had remained empty, and his plate overloaded with all the delicacies. As long as Grandfather lived, no-one was allowed to touch the food.

They were not David, grandfather used to say, whom the Lord had allowed to eat from the showbread of the temple. They were certainly not on the run or in times of famine, like the widow who had prepared a meal from the last of the oil and flour for the prophet Elijah and not for her own son.

Which brings us back to Elijah.

Elijah the prophet was strict, grandfather used to say, like the Lord who reaps where He had not sown. When Elijah came, he would demand an account for every single year, an explanation of what they had done with his sumptuous plate.

Sure, the meal could have been given to the poor, but Elijah was Old Testament. An eye for an eye, a tooth for a tooth, it seemed more appropriate not to give the meal to anyone. To bury it in a deep hole, to give it back to Mother Earth, where it ultimately came from and where every mortal body would end up.

At that time, Grandfather had no idea that people would come up with the idea of shooting their ashes, or later even their entire dead body, into space in packages, thus calling into question the old saying: You are earth, you must return to earth.

He would have been surprised at many things, but now he was lying in the dead earth, not far from the place where they had buried Elijah's untouched food every year. Perhaps grandfather had also been a reincarnated pharaoh, who had only made sure to hide the most delicious food in the ground while he was still alive, before he himself followed into the realm of the dead. Then it was pretty mean to break this tradition, because at some point the supplies would be used up, and then what would become of grandfather? Everything was just a fraction of the thoughts that arose in the family when grandfather died. What should be done with the tradition? Even within the family, there were revolutionaries who even called for the tradition to be abandoned completely. Why leave the door open, there was only a draught while they ate the food. And anyway, Elijah could knock when he came. Why put down an empty plate, leave an unoccupied seat, it was far too crowded at the table anyway. Fortunately, they, the revolutionaries in the family, couldn't get their way.

Someone had suggested that Elijah had ascended to heaven in a fiery chariot. Who could guarantee that he wouldn't race through our house in this fiery vehicle in a rage when he found the door locked, no chair free, no plate heaped with delicacies. If he really came at some point. And nobody had any doubts about that in their hearts.

So, a compromise was reached. Everything went on as before, except that Elijah's food was simply put in the kitchen in the evening so that a decision could be made the next day on what to do with it. And every year this decision was invalid the next morning, either Elijah had appeared in disguise(?) in the night when everyone was already asleep, or, and the downcast expressions on the faces of some family members tended to suggest this, there had been a whole mass migration in the kitchen during the night. Which also explained why some of them had eaten suspiciously little the night before, obviously knowing that the actual feast would not take place until the midnight celebration.

The remains of the meal were worth nothing more than being buried. This meant that bad times had also dawned for grandfather: instead of the annual Elijah-rich feast, only gnawed bones and the bitter peel of the otherwise delicious fruit reached him underground. Times were getting harder, even for the dead.

Which brings us back to burying.

Grandfather loved the Old Testament Bible, but had sometimes ventured into New Testament territory. He particularly liked the example of the talents. Especially because it expressed a certain Old Testament rigor. The Lord reaps where He does not sow, those who had a lot, got more, those who had nothing had the rest taken away from them. In any case, a superficial interpretation of this story would lead to that conclusion.

The first two were of little interest to me, who in their life is so richly blessed as to have five talents? Five real talents. And don't the richly blessed tend to let their talents atrophy because everything comes far too easily to them until they wake up and realize that a talent needs to be doubled with hard work in order to blossom fully?

Two talents seemed more realistic to me, but who manages to double what they have in their lifetime – some overshoot the mark, end up with tenfold, a thousandfold accumulation, but times had become hard not only for the dead grandfather, the generation, that had amassed a multiple wealth in passing, lay like grandfather in the lap of Mother Earth. And the others had an unspeakable struggle to preserve the talents that had saved the family from the jaws of the state,

A talent. And someone who would demand accountability. That seemed appropriate for the times. I thought about it. With speculation I could get ten times as much. What would the Lord say if I gave him ten back instead of one? A stale aftertaste rose up in me. Of course He would want to know how I had done it. The journey was the reward.

Speculating, I would have to answer meekly, risk business, financial Russian roulette.

And what would He think if I had risked everything and lost?

Lord, burying it was out of the question for me. Not because of Grandpa, he didn't need any more money; the money was safe in the ground, no dead person would touch it, with death the money had become what it was, worthless funny printed paper, worthless metal that had escaped the scrap dealer.

Nevertheless, burying it was out of the question, I knew the Lord's answer when I dug a hole in the ground next to my grandfather in front of the Almighty, took out the talent and it was no more than before.

Speculate and misspeculate, what if I told Him: The banks are big crooks. They take 15%, Lord, but only give 2% if you bring it to them. You must understand that I couldn't take it to the bank. 2% minus inflation, Lord, I couldn't have come before you. And besides, Lord, these are difficult times I live in. The state is dead as a doornail, bankrupt, it doesn't matter, life goes on. But now even the banks are dead as a doornail, how can it go on, how could I put the money in the bank? So, it didn't matter, Lord, better to speculate, all or nothing, well, nothing happened, but you have to understand, it could have been anything. It could have turned out differently.

I felt the penetrating gaze of the Lord, because there was no other way.

You made it far too easy for yourself, grandfather, how often did you tell me your favorite story, and when I began to understand a tiny detail, you withdrew comfortably, let yourself have a good time with Elijah's meal and left me alone with a thousand and one questions. And one question, Lord, five talents, two talents, one talent. What about the number 0, why did you create the number 0? Are there people with zero talents? I mean, at the beginning, not at the end, after the reckoning.

I thought of the people I knew. I couldn't think of anyone. I didn't know a real zero. Not a zero, Lord. Grandfather's image appeared before my eyes. Also the picture of the Lord as I had seen it earlier in my children's Bible.

There is no zero, Grandpa said, in eight billion people you won't find a single zero.

The Lord smiled. No zero, He repeated, not before the reckoning and not after the reckoning.

These are the feasts of the LORD, even holy convocations, which ye shall proclaim in their seasons. In the fourteenth day of the first month at even is the LORD's passover. And on the fifteenth day of the same month is the feast of unleavened bread unto the LORD: seven days ye must eat unleavened bread.
(Levitikus 23: 4-6)

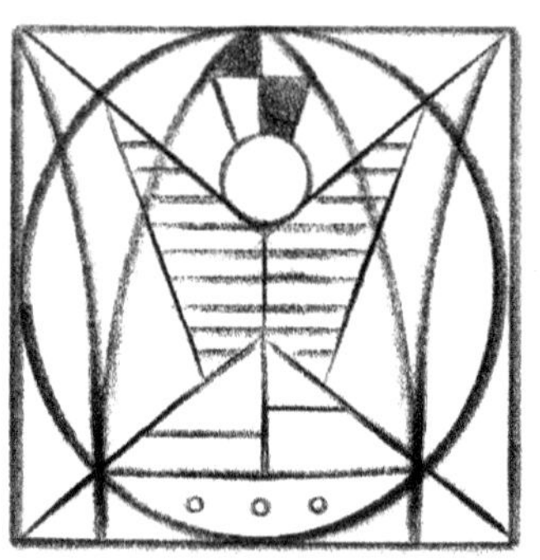

8.
The Smallest Greatest

Cars, airplanes and, especially, trains. Everything fascinated this little Jakob. He had seen hundreds of city trains. Nevertheless. When he was visiting and we were sitting at the dining table, regardless of whether it was quiet or a conversation was taking place, a city train whizzed past our window, the track was less than 30 meter away, Jakob jumped up and shouted:

Look, a train, with a red roof, red, I rode on one of those.

His voice was full of excitement. When the train was gone, he poked listlessly at his potatoes again, as if nothing special had happened.

I have forgotten about fire departments. Fire engines were the crowning glory of his mobile objects of fascination. In America, I had been photographed next to one of these vehicles; like everything else in this country, it was gigantic, as long as a block of houses. The huge fire engine lay dormant on a photo CD, poor Jakob, there are also disadvantages to digital photography, every time I visited, he reminded me to finally print out the photo.

Life mostly consists of detours. To get to heaven, we first go back to earth, as if we had to cross the dark globe once at the end of our lives in order to come out at the other end and be able to ascend to heaven.

Elijah had an easier time.

He was one of the few who left this earth without any detours. Where was this event recorded in the thick old book? In Kings of course, such a royal event can only be written in Kings.

As they were walking along and talking together, suddenly a chariot of fire and horses of fire appeared and separated the two of them, and Elijah went up to heaven in a whirlwind. Elisha saw this and cried out, My father! My father! The chariots and horsemen of Israel! And Elisha saw him no more. Then he took hold of his garment and tore it in two. Elisha then picked up Elijah's cloak that had fallen from him and went back and stood on the bank of the Jordan.

(2 Kings 2:11-13)

When I read this story again in the old book, I realized why it was reserved for Elijah. He was described as the driver of a chariot. Elijah was one of the few who had a license to drive a fiery chariot with fiery horses. And not only did he have such a license, he was also much better at it than the license indicated. This at least was one reason why Elijah was allowed to go straight to heaven in a fiery chariot.

In a fiery chariot. What would Jakob have said? The sight of a fiery chariot. No fire engine, no airplane, no train, what would Jakob have...

In 20 years, grown up, having grown up in Germany, he might have asked:

Does it even have an operating license? And there is no TÜV (official technical certification) seal to be seen. What if an airplane crossed its path?

A few hundred kilometers further west, a Frenchman might have said:

Fabulous. But why be in such a hurry. First, a leisurely glass of wine.

Quite different, even though we're talking about the same fiery chariot.

A Russian might have remarked:

Our cosmonauts were in space and didn't find God. Where is he going?

And an Englishman? Probably:

Great horses, I'd like to know what concentrated feed he's feeding them.

The Americans probably wouldn't be embarrassed either:

Great performance, they would say, but is he faster than our Saturn rockets? If not, we could try to catch up with him and subject him to questioning.

And the Italians:

Too bad. He's missing his funeral. We would have given him such a nice funeral.

An Irishman? I don't know, maybe he would have been surprised that roads are already being built in the air.

And an Arab?

The horse droppings must be made of gold, like with Aladdin.

Questions, lots of questions, even more guesses. Jakob, my little boy with his cars, airplanes and trains. Jakob is standing in a field, flowers everywhere, and in front of him the prophet Elijah is ascending to heaven in a fiery chariot drawn by horses. What would he have said as a child, not yet grown out of childhood?

I'm sure he would have jumped up out of excitement, at least as excited, if a city train had rattled past our window.

Great, can I go for a ride? I have to put on an astronaut suit first, it must be pretty hot in a fiery chariot.

Can I go for a ride?

It's the only logical reaction to the sight of a fiery chariot ascending into the sky. What's a Saturn rocket, a Concord or any other supersonic airplane, a Rolls Royce or a mile-long fire engine when you can ride in a fiery chariot?

Great, can I come along?

The prophet Elijah would certainly have turned around, despite all the haste, because it was the question of a child. He would have turned around, smiled at Jakob and answered:

I am going to heaven, Jakob, to God. You are a little child, and the little children, Jakob, they are already with God, alive in heaven, even if they are on Earth.

Elijah roared off with golden sparks and Jakob, although he was sad because he had missed his ride, nevertheless beamed because he had understood Elijah's answer, because Jakob was still a small child.

At that time the disciples came to Jesus and asked, Who, then, is the greatest in the kingdom of heaven?

He called a little child to him and placed the child among them. And he said: Truly I tell you, unless you change and become like little children, you will never enter the kingdom of heaven. Therefore, whoever takes the lowly position of this child is the greatest in the kingdom of heaven. (Matthew 18:1-4)

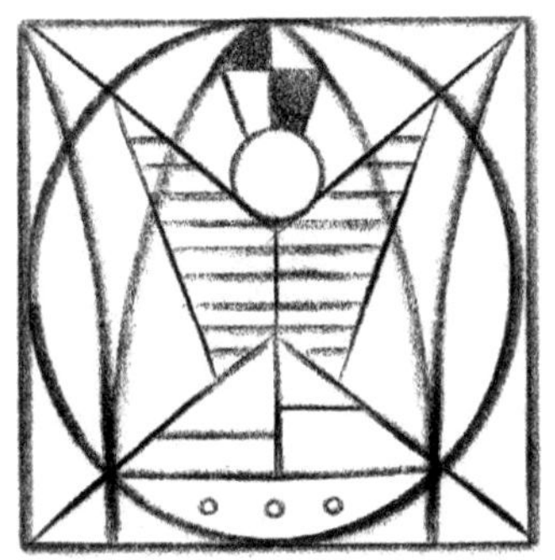

9.

Watery Fire

Then said Elijah unto the people, I, even I only, remain a prophet of the LORD; but Baal's prophets are four hundred and fifty men.

Let them therefore give us two bullocks; and let them choose one bullock for themselves, and cut it in pieces, and lay it on wood, and put no fire under: and I will dress the other bullock, and lay it on wood, and put no fire under:

And call ye on the name of your gods, and I will call on the name of the LORD: and the God that answereth by fire, let him be God. And all the people answered and said, It is well spoken.

(1 Kings 18: 22-24)

Then the fire of the LORD fell, and consumed the burnt sacrifice, and the wood, and the stones, and the dust, and licked up the water that was in the trench.

And when all the people saw it, they fell on their faces: and they said, The LORD, he is the God; the LORD, he is the God.

(1 Kings 18:38, 39)

As a child, some strange associations come to one's mind. The dance of the Baal priests reminds me of the story from Africa, with a huge pot in the middle in which an unsuspecting stranger is being cooked. The only thing that unites them is the dance around a center. Around a giant cooking pot or a huge wooden pyre. And here was the problem. No fire. The priests of Baal could dance as wildly as they wanted, their idols would not listen to them, they did not send a fire to consume the meal prepared for them. And Elijah. He must have sat quietly in a corner, watching the strange goings-on. But that was not all. He goaded the others on.

Shout louder, perhaps your idols won't hear because they are asleep.

The others shouted louder. Wiped their skin bloody with knives, bloody, ecstasy, in vain, how could they bring dead creatures, the work of human hands, back to life.

I can do that too.

It was many years ago. A normal country circus. In the middle, a magician performing tricks. Children's eyes everywhere, wide with amazement.

Until suddenly a little boy shouted out:

I can do that too!

And the magician? What was he supposed to do? Ignore the voice? Distract him with an even better trick? What if the boy shouted again: I can do that too? Let him prove it, even if it was a humiliation, but there was a chance that he was a little show-off. Perhaps he wouldn't dare enter the circus ring. And even then, the brat would fail miserably in front of everyone; it had taken him, the great magician, many years to rehearse this trick.

What would Elijah have said if the priests of Baal had gotten the pyre to burn, fanned only by a wild dance? Were they not also connected to powers? Pharaoh's priests hurled their staffs to the ground and they turned into snakes just like Moses' staff. Up to that point there was equality of arms.

Only, Moses' serpent swallowed Pharaoh's serpents. A clear sign. But one fire cannot consume another and if both had produced a flame, the people would hardly have been impressed just because Elijah's flame was a few centimeters higher.

But Elijah remained calm. A cool situation. Two were competing, vying for the same girl. A situation that is common in the animal kingdom. A test of courage. The same for everyone. And the girl looks on, watches and waits to see who passes the test. And you see your rival and you know one hundred percent: he won't make it. The woman, the people, are yours.

But why take the humiliation to the extreme? The priests of Baal had failed. Carved themselves into ecstasy without the pile catching fire. And Elijah? Why didn't he just snap his fingers, he knew the power behind him. Pour water over the wood. Of course he did. It was far too easy to light a pile of wood without fire. It had to be a wet woodpile. Or was that the trick?

Later, in the New Testament, Christ turned water into wine. Of course he did. Elijah had water lit and on the way the water turned into methylated spirits. The hot desert sun would do the rest.

No wine, no methylated spirits, the most precious thing there was in the desert, water, to make a miracle even greater.

Why? O Lord, what a stiff-necked people you have chosen. What miracles you showed them, in the end they were hardly impressed. The parted sea, flying snakes, manna, quails, the rock that gave water, you get used to everything.

And Elijah? Like the Lord, Elijah knew the bride he was courting. Elijah placed a pane of glass in the woodpile, a burning glass. The sun lit the fire. Simple calculation. They would find many explanations, even if the appointed fire expert had sifted through the pile of ashes in vain for a shard of glass.

Pour water over the wood. Pour the most precious thing you have in the desert and I will give you greater things. More than water in the desert. A fire that burns in your heart.

Elijah's face resembled a face carved out of rock. Strong, unaffected, no uncertain twitches in any corner. The water of the desert was the oil in his fire.

I can do that too. Not a voice was raised, although many stood in a large circle around the fire, many, including children.

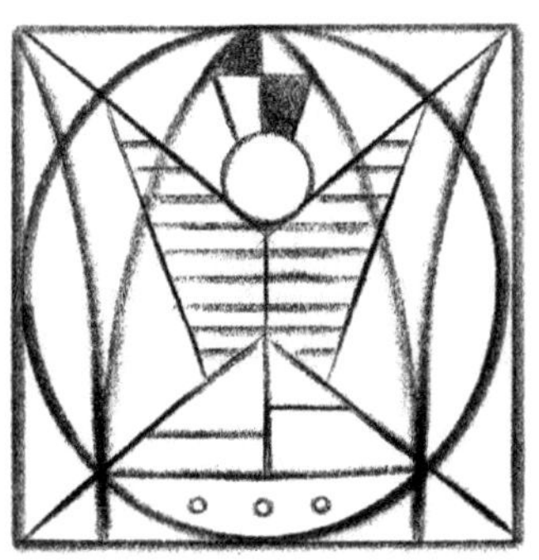

10.

The Lost Sinner

No, it wasn't under the table. I had already looked. Maybe I had overlooked it. Impossible. There was a small cavity under the table leg. Maybe it had slipped down. I had searched everything, photographed it with the flashlight. Even under the feet? Yes, no, not at all. I don't mean all the feet. It was exhausting to crawl under the low table. I was no longer fully focused on the last table leg. I had to check at least the last one.

Which was the last one? I had searched under the table four times, statistically every table leg could have been the last one. Or the other way round, once the first, particularly thoroughly searched. My back. It was aching. All the bending over. I crawled under the table like a dog. Breadcrumbs. When was the last time I'd vacuumed? Yesterday. But my son had vacuumed. Statistically speaking, every crumb of bread under our dining table had a better chance of surviving when he sucked. The crumbs stuck to my hands. Lick them off? What confused thoughts come to one's mind under a dark table. It had been 30 years since I was allowed to be under a table. I was soon too old for that. Who likes having their legs cut off, besides, it wasn't appropriate for many reasons.

Was it worth the effort to crawl under the table again? It could have fallen out of his pocket on the way. Somewhere in a puddle of rain, run over by hundreds of cars. My little piece of paper. With the important phone number. Why was I actually looking for it? Maybe I can remember the number...

Something shimmers white at the back, the last table leg. Damn, I hit my head. No rush. That white something won't get away from you. Finally, why did I overlook the note the other times? Anyway, all's well that ends well...

All bad. Nothing again. A trivial scrap of paper, no numbers. No telephone number. Who throws scraps of paper on the floor here? I could still understand pogroms. But paper? No order. Always my speech. Nobody thinks, not for a moment. Not under the table, not even on the sofa. Where had I been for the last hour?

In the kitchen – of course. I was in the kitchen half the time. Why not think first? Typical. Crawling under the table five times without any rhyme or reason instead of checking in the kitchen

But the note was still in my pocket when I left the kitchen. Of course it was. There was jam on my fingers, so I didn't want to take it out, but I had clearly seen the tip sticking out of my pocket when my sticky fingers reached for the white paper. Remember.

The first number was a four. I can see it clearly in front of me. A four, right at the front of the number line. Right at the front. Didn't it start with a five? I was still wondering why the number started with a five. Of course it did. That's how it was. The five at the front. Then the four was in second place. 54. 54.

The structure looked strange. I didn't remember the lost piece of paper, the lost phone number. I had to leave in a few minutes. No, I'll cancel everything, I have to find that note. It must be somewhere, it can't have dissolved. Not even in a puddle. I saw it sticking out of my pocket in the kitchen. That's why I didn't put it in properly?

Damn. A thumbtack was stuck in my hand, I was still crawling on all fours under the table and had started to lift the corners of the carpet. Who on earth drops a thumbtack without picking it up? Anger rose up inside me. Beethoven must have known what this story reminded him of. Anger over the lost penny. A perpetuum mobile of somersaulting notes. Over and over, mixed up, wild like a small hurricane. Not in the kitchen, not on the sofa. Nothing here under the carpet either.

The bookshelf. Perhaps I had placed it on the edge of a shelf. Perhaps in front of a novel entitled: Man's Search for Happiness. Or: World Travel in the 20th Century, or rather Domestic World Travel in the 20th Century.

No matter in front of which book. The note could only be on the bookshelf, of course, or, maybe still, yes, I hadn't been in the bathroom, I mean, not to look for the note before.

I'll find it, and if I turn everything upside down, the bookshelf, the bathroom, somewhere...

Or suppose a woman has ten silver coins and loses one. Doesn't she light a lamp, sweep the house and search carefully until she finds it? And when she finds it, she calls her friends and

neighbors together and says, 'Rejoice with me; I have found my lost coin.' In the same way, I tell you, there is rejoicing in the presence of the angels of God over one sinner who repents.
(Luke 15:8-10)

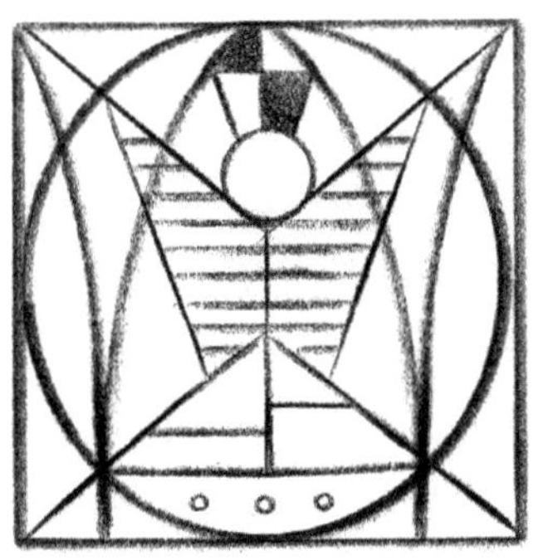

11.
(Not) Guilty Guilt/Grace

A disaster. What a disaster. At first, he had a bad feeling. Be that as it may, he was not a gut person. Reason led him to another decision. The end result was disaster. The first department had already been dissolved, two others were swaying like reeds in the midst of increasingly frequent winds of climate catastrophe.

His decisions had been good so far, but not as accurate as his predecessor, who would now be sizzling in the sun on some island before heading off to the GP for his next screening check-up. He did not have the courage of his predecessor to make unusual decisions, nor did he have the strength or will to push them through against all odds.

So far, however, his decisions on the latest fashion trends had led to annual, albeit smaller, profits for the company. Until now. Now was not until now, now was disaster, now was catastrophe, now was the closure of departments. Just because he had once been more than totally wrong in his assessment. Trend, zeitgeist, fashion, more than totally wrongly assessed, vast quantities of goods wrongly ordered, now dangling on stands in stores, hardly any bought.

The door opened. Relief, not his boss but Ms. Sommter, the secretary.

The boss sends his apologies. He has been delayed. It'll take a little longer. I think you can guess why, she added pointedly.

That old cow, he thought. Acting like she's the boss. Cheap typist, computer typist, his thoughts followed, while he smiled at her kindly.

Thank you.

That was all his tongue could manage. Unsalivated, it stuck to his dry palate while little rivulets rushed over his damp palms. The pandemic came towards him. Everything was at a distance. As was the reality anyway. But now officially. No greeting with a handshake when his boss entered. The clammy hands might give him away. Thanks to the pandemic. He had a better grip on his face, although you have a grip on your hands. His face was also closer to his head, the control center of his aging body. No sweat on his forehead, no flushing.

Why of all things were his hands going crazy? Was it stress? Ms. Sommter had disappeared. He imagined her second appearance when his boss would excuse himself once again.

Second act, first teeth. Typist's entrance: fast, confident gait. Head up, nose even higher, lips pursed, contempt disguised behind pity in her eyes.

It wouldn't come to that. He jumped up, a thousandth of a second before the door opened, pumped air into the depths of his black lungs, opened his mouth, his damp right hand clenched into a fist...

Please stay seated, a deep voice echoed.

His boss was a head taller, a broad, square body on two thin legs; under a tangled bush of eyebrows, two poisonous green eyes stabbed at him.

Sit down, my good man, echoed the deep voice, we all need to sit down more, slow down, meditate, take our time.

He looked around as if to see in which corner of the room these words had originated.

I'll be brief. The whole thing went bloody wrong. It cost me my lunch break to appease the board. Some wanted heads to roll. Luckily, we're at war. Enough heads are rolling in the media. You don't need any more. Thanks to the war. Never mind, thank whoever you want. For all I care, thank the office chair you're glued to. Which won't let you go so it doesn't have to get used to another butt.

His boss laughed, he tried to do the same, laughed at his own butt. He had never liked it anyway. When he was at school, he only wore clothes that hung like a curtain over his butt, which in his eyes, although they had never seen this part of his body, stuck out horribly and misshapenly into the surroundings.

His classmates had noticed it. They didn't talk about it, but he felt it. One day, a triviality that he would nonetheless never forget, the class ran up a flight of stairs, the boy running behind him suddenly grabbed the hem of his anorak and tugged it upwards. What was he expecting, a covered crater-shaped hole, a bulge the size of a soccer ball protruding outwards?

He had stumbled forward, everyone paused for a split second, every tongue was silent, briefly, too briefly, before loud laughter erupted.

I will be brief. The boss interrupted his thoughts searching through the past. We'll chop it off. Period.

He felt relieved and wanted to hold out his sweaty hand to his boss.

Heinrich, the cart's breaking, his boss burst out.

A moment of silence, his mind raced, what did this senseless remark mean? Fortunately, he remembered the fairy tale before he was embarrassed.

Yes, he stammered, the tire of my heart. It burst with a bang.

A tire, his boss thundered. Mount Everest fell off your heart. A little more gratitude, just a little, I suppose I can expect that.

Stammering, he apologized for his big mistake.

Thank you, to the falling Mount Everest, 8000 thank you's, thank you, thank you, thank you, thank you, I don't know how...

Enough, interrupted his boss, I don't have to suffer second-hand thanks.

His boss's eyes flashed to the door; he left the room backwards in a stooped posture. His subservient spirit had not expected this. The debt forgiven. A second chance. A new start.

Everything to zero. A new liberated beginning. No burden. No guilt.

Without changing his stooped posture, he returned to his own office. His back fell into the hollow of his chair, which had been pressed in for years. Closing his eyes, he enjoyed his burden-free shoulders. The third time he heard the knock. Not a brisk one, rather timid, uncertain.

He knew how to read the knock like a handshake.

Come in, he said firmly.

The door struggled to open from the latched handle. One of his subordinates squeezed his body through the crack in the door.

What is it, Miller, he asked challengingly.

The small spark of wind, the courage with which he had ventured here, escaped from the other's sails.

It's about the report, Miller stammered. I'm not, but my wife is ill, the children, taking them to school, cooking, I have...

He interrupted his stammering.

What about the report? he shouted. Not finished? How dare you come in here and look me in the eye like that!

His voice broke. His face flaming red, his body rose from the chair, the familiar hollow he had personally made over the years.

I'm terribly sorry, Miller stuttered, I'll be working every night to finish...

You're not going to do anything, he interrupted. The company has taken a huge hit and you, you come to me with nothing, nothing.

My children, my wife, Miller stammered, they're not nothing, they're, they're...

They are, they are, he hissed back. You're nothing but a failure. Right now. It depends on everyone. On everything. Nothing must go wrong. And you, you come to me with your trivial private matters.

He snorted. His hands dug into the table like a vice. Miller backed away. His glittering eyes caught up with him, pinning him to the floor.

This is inexcusable, he said in a suddenly quiet voice, triumphant in its undertone. Not with me, Miller. Not like this. Not anymore. Never again. You're fired. Now. Pack your things. Get out of here right now.

You can't do that, Miller replied. My wife is not healthy, three children have to...

You want to tell me what I can and can't do, he roared abruptly. How dare you. It's already come to that.

He picked up the phone and his secretary answered.

Ms. Hendryk. Bring me the termination form BO2AR. Yes, for immediate dismissal. Enter the name Miller. Then bring it to my office immediately.

Less than five minutes later, the paper was shaking in Miller's hands.

Escort Miller to his office, he ordered his secretary. He has ten minutes to pack his things. Then accompany him to the exit. And instruct the porter to block Miller's access card immediately.

I, I know what I can do, Miller, he shouted after the man. Not with me. Not like this anymore. Time to finally clean out this mess. An old era had dawned anew.

The servant's master took pity on him, canceled the debt and let him go. But when that servant went out, he found one of his fellow servants who owed him a hundred silver coins. He grabbed him and began to choke him. 'Pay back what you owe me!' he demanded. His fellow

servant fell to his knees and begged him, 'Be patient with me, and I will pay it back.' But he refused. Instead, he went off and had the man thrown into prison until he could pay the debt.
(Matthew 18:27-30)

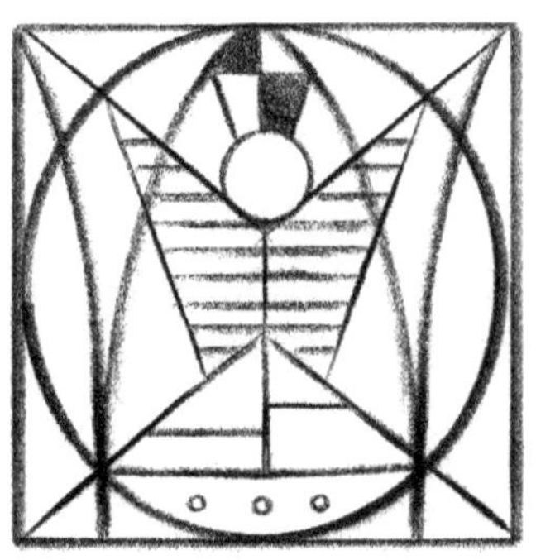

12.
Odd Packaging

Determined but a little uncertain, he headed towards the bookshop. A glance through the window revealed: no other customers. It simplified his business. He entered the store, heavy bells above him that went into a deep trance-like vibration when he opened the door. Next to the till, an old man, engrossed in an even older book. His eyes circled the store, nowhere a young, pretty sales clerk. He would have to deal with the old man, at least if he wasn't hard of hearing, if he didn't have to speak so loudly that a conversation could be heard on the street.
He pulled out his thick wallet and dropped it next to the old book. Thick clouds of dust whirled upwards, the old man sneezed violently, his monocle shattered a thousand times over when it hit the counter.

I'm sorry, he apologized. Wanted to reassure you from the start. I'm sure you belong to our town's Heart Needs Peace group.

Motionless, a little defiant, the old man gazed at him unwaveringly, hypnotized, unable to avert his eyes.

He just wanted to make it clear from the outset:

Money doesn't matter. Hence the wallet. I think you understand what my words are trying to convey to your brain.

The old man was still staring at him, no old words crept out of his dry tongue through the gaps in his teeth.

I'd like half a kilo of adventure novel. The most important thing, he mumbled. Before that, five pages of a romance novel, from the back please, it's not so tough there and three pages from an art book to start with. With photos from Europe please, preferably northern Italy, it's the most digestible.

The old man had written everything down.

Do you have stomach problems? he asked in a low voice, or perhaps heartburn, a little higher up in the head?

He shook his head.

Thankfully not.

Then you could also do with a war novel, said the old man. Something hearty and altogether more cutting.

He reached behind him for a book, stretched out his arm and weighed the book in his hand.

Unfortunately, 622 grams, the old man burst out. What did you say, half a kilo?
He nodded.

I used to be a world champion at estimating weights. To the nearest microgram. Today, unfortunately, only to a thousandth of a gram. A part of my senses has left me, who knows where to.
He never thought that everything would be taken for granted.

It's hearty but not too spicy. 14 individual and 325 battlefield deaths. It's from the Middle Ages. You can digest something like that. Something from the First or even the Second World War is so stomach-churning that it is no longer in demand.
He thought about it. Would a crime novel be more palatable?

I did too, the old man interrupted him.
He could obviously read minds. He reached behind him again.

How did you like your steak in the past? the old man wanted to know, blue rare, rare, medium rare, medium or a little well done?

His thoughts took a huge leap into the past, no memory, none of his brain circuits still contained memory atoms of a rare or well-done steak. Books galore. That wasn't a problem. But there he preferred...

Here I have a well-done thriller, the old man interrupted his thoughts again. Only poison murders. No knives, no accidents, no guns, not a drop of blood. If you prefer well done. Otherwise, I advise you – he reached for another copy – to read this book. Murder weapons only knives and other sharp objects, if you used to like blood more.
He shook his head.

Thank you for your efforts. I'll stick to 500 grams of adventure novel. Plus, three pages of romance novels, not American ones please, too sweet and no English pilchered ones either – I can do what I like here and never got any tingling exotic flavor into it. The pages from the photo documentation as you wrote it down. That is all. With practiced movements, the old man tore an adventure novel in half, cutting 500 grams out of the middle. He also skillfully retrieved the other wishes from two dark book entrails.

He disappeared briefly behind a curtain and returned with a lump of ham in his left hand. In his right hand he held a millennia-old Japanese samurai sword. Before he realized, the old man was cutting millimeter-thin slices of ham with the sword.

I wrap everything in ham. Don't look skeptical. You only get the best goods anyway. The ham imparts a little more flavor, some presentations are admittedly a little dry. All you have to do is confirm in writing that you will dispose of the ham packaging in the special garbage can provided. Unfortunately, there are fellow citizens, the eternally incorrigible, who still consume old packaging and not the new products. With the comforting feeling of holding the damp packaging in his hands, he left the bookshop in silence. He had to hurry. Half of his lunch break had already disappeared into the dark bookshop.

No-one sews a patch of unshrunk cloth on an old garment, for the patch will pull away from the garment, making the tear worse. Neither do people pour new wine into old wineskins. If they do, the skins will burst; the wine will run out and the wineskins will be ruined. No, they pour new

wine into new wineskins, and both are preserved.
(Matthew 9:16,17)

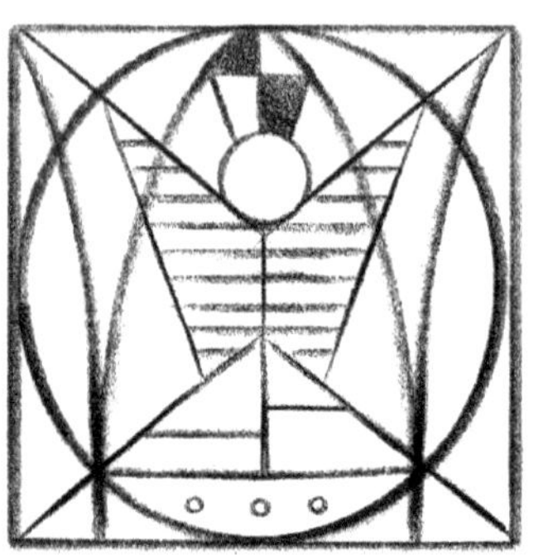

13.

Participating listener

For over half an hour, the masses of sound had been flooding through the concert hall. The waves of string bows rolled through the room, flutes ignited a glittering, sparkling cloud of bright tonal lights. Before the steady rise and fall of the string waves turned into a tiring uniformity, huge cascades erupted from the trombones at irregular intervals, their dark bells resembling the open mouth of a greedy predator. In a few places, the music seemed to fall asleep, only a few single string pizzicati played short notes that disappeared silently into the darkness of the hall in the next moment, soft drums murmured, a sleeping brook moved almost motionlessly through a lost landscape, short breaths from the bassoon and oboe rumbled strange noises into the room, coming from invisible animal throats. It had been thirty minutes, it no longer counted, the dark murmur of the drums had long since increased steadily into frightening, increasingly aggressive loud beats. The strange bassoon and oboe sounds changed with every second into pained, screaming maws, torn from the flesh of their bodies, which sometimes stumbled, sometimes raced through the dark clouds of sound in confused convulsions. The simultaneous rise and fall of the string bows, still perfect despite their increasing ferocity, became a mighty tsunami front, towering threateningly in front of the moat that protected them from the motionless staring spectators.

A deep groan escaped from the trombones, the trumpets shattered the remaining silent islands above the musicians' heads. Meanwhile, eight hands were beating the drums and timpani incessantly and wildly. The uncontrolled sound wafted along the edge of an invisible wall that separated it from the horrified listeners, ready at any moment to break everything down and sweep it away.

He was still sitting quietly in his seat. For over 30 years. Not just for this piece. For many. But especially this one. Hardly any of them had this crazy, furious finale, in which all the catastrophes that had befallen this world had come together one last time for the expected final catastrophic apocalypse. His eyes fixed on the drummers. They beat the dead animal skins in unmeasurable whirls of vibration.

Next to them, he spotted his two actual targets. A black tailcoat, clutching two bronze cymbals and pushing them upwards against the clouds of sound weighing down on them. Next to him was another black tailcoat, a hammer in his hand, his arm already spread wide to smash the instrument onto the gong at the very last second, to put a final and irrefutable end to this crazy world with this single blow.

He looked briefly at the conductor's face. Behind closed eyes, the jumbled coils of his brain drove both arms, which alternately struck the various instrument groups and drove the chaos towards the abyss. His leg muscles tensed, the score appeared before his eyes.

Inwardly he counted the seconds, trying to harmonize them with the uncoordinated twitching of the conductor's arms. The cymbals had reached the intended height, in five seconds they would deafen what was not yet deafened with a deafening noise, collapsing over musicians, instruments, conductors, the hall, the whole world, united with the collapsing wall of sound that would be torn from its foundations by the hammer on the gong.

Three seconds, he trembled, every muscle fiber oscillated, his heavy upper body fought against his legs to keep them on the ground.

One last second. It was silent as the grave inside him, huge heavy masses of sound piled up above him, he did not hear a single sound from this threatening primal mass. All the wild structures in his head were switched off. What came next was automatism, performed hundreds of times, perfected each time.

The two arms covered in a tailcoat struck each other deafeningly at the conductor's last signal, at the same moment the heavy mallet struck the gong, a huge final wave of sound broke from the metal of the instrument and crashed into the walls of sound of the trombones.

Everything somersaulted over the petrified heads of the audience. Not even a hundredth of a second after the final rushing chord, his legs jerked upwards. A huge, dark hole burst in the grimace of his face and his throat let out a long, drawn-out braaaaavoooo. A millisecond's pause, followed by a second bravoo, more focused, louder, aimed directly at the conductor.

In the meantime, his feet had landed on the ground again, and once more even the smallest muscle in his limbs tensed up and flung his body upwards once more.

Bravooo, bravo, incessantly, one more time, one more time, he was still floating, bravo, bravo, the pauses became shorter with each shout, now his hands slapped together in loud applause with each shout. Braaavooooo.

Behind him sat a child, looking with confused eyes at the bouncing, screaming creature. When it turned to its mother questioningly, she looked helplessly to the side, confused.

Before the child's eyes, the bouncing body sank back down. At the moment when his feet hit the floor, not from the impact, his head bowed forward in homage, as if the thunderous applause was only for him, not for the conductor, not for the musicians, not for the instruments, not for the composers, not for anyone else, just for him. For no-one at that moment could show in his mind that moment of unconditional self-abandonment, even if it only served to draw the roar of the storm of applause to him, to draw all eyes to his excited facade, which alone was worthy of such a manifestation.

They tie up heavy, cumbersome loads and put them on other people's shoulders, but they themselves are not willing to lift a finger to move them. Everything they do is done for people to see: they make their phylacteries wide and the tassels on their garments long; they love the place of honor at banquets and the most important seats in the synagogues; they love to be greeted with respect in the marketplaces and to be called 'Rabbi' by others.
(Matthew 23:4-7)

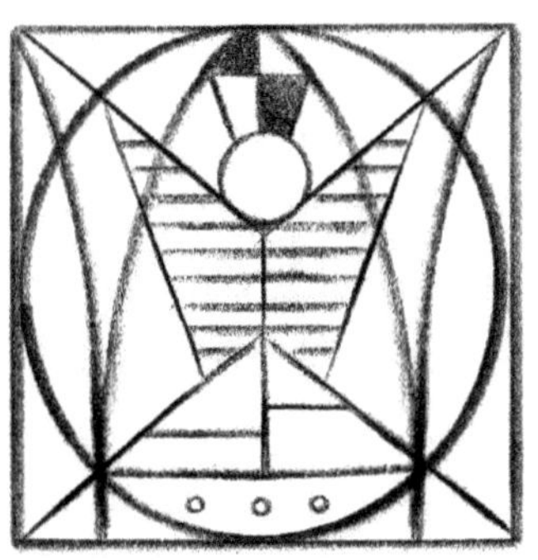

14.
Miracles in disguise

The sand was smoking. Gray, crushed air steamed through the rows, mixing with the body odors of those present and the half-full beer glasses. Those who weren't chatting were trying to follow the speaker. Chunks of words penetrated the hanging air, the voice of a spirit coming from deep inside a mountain.

We will solve problems. Everything. Everything will be better. Only we ... the others ... dirt, finally we have to clean up.

Strangely, the scraps of words joined together. A corpulent man stood on the podium. His face was glowing fiery red, and rivulets of sweat were pouring from his forehead, some of which ran into a beer glass in front of him.

He was right. He embodies something of life. He will clean up. No more sloppiness. He'll have to build a lot of new prisons. The others will envy us. Finally, the longed-for savior.

The people were satisfied. Their satisfaction was a mixture of smoke, beer and hope, in which the puffed-up bright star of a man shone. They had seen him, who had come to make everything right again.

There were candles in every corner of the room, giving off a spicy smell. Carpets adorned the wall, with small Buddha figures in front of some of them. In the middle of the room was a bed-like structure. And in the middle of the structure, in other words right in the center of the aura, sat a haggard figure. Legs knotted in a cross-legged position, eyes fixed on the infinite nothingness.

Around the bed-like structure with the haggard figure sat about 20 people. Gender, age, appearance, all different, mixed together. When the word water was spoken, they stood up and moved to a counter-like table, overloaded with bottles of water. Two scantily clad women stood behind it, smiled, never stopped smiling and handed out the healing water – for a reasonable charge, which they placed in a velvet-lined casket.

After drinking the water, the people returned to their seats. The gaunt figure had straightened up. The gnarled feet stood on a pool of broken glass. The figure's eyes were wide open, hugely dilated pupils, magically attracting the gaze of those present to see an ancient tree of life blooming pink behind it. The way there, only he could guide them, they knew it now even more than at the beginning of the media digitization.

The body was twisted into strange contortions. Arms intertwined like a web, legs cramped together, bent hard against the body. Ever-changing grimaces ran across the face, involuntary, driven by an unknown, invisible force.

A huge crowd was waiting outside. The chain moved patiently forward, disappeared link by link into the small house and was spat out again at the back. With glazed eyes, many of them, beams on their faces, tears rolling down the wrinkled valleys of old faces. Changed, that had changed, not yet the other thing they had come for. It needed time. Not that important. For someone who had dragged himself around with an illness for ten years, the time of the journey home didn't mean much. That's what the boy's father had said. You have to believe. Only believe until you are home. Then you will see the miracle in your body.

And because their faith was so weak, they had bought some of the miracle water, which had become miraculous because the boy with the skewed eyes bathed in this pool every day. Faith was important. They were allowed to supplement the rest with the miracle water. And the time. Just wait until they were home. No more pain. Legs that bounced through the street like deer again. Paralyzed arms that would turn into body-builder exhibits. Waiting until the journey home. Hadn't the Lord also said to the supplicant: *Go home. There you will find your servant in good health.* Waiting for home.

The chain did not get any shorter. Expectant faces disappeared into the house and returned to daylight at the back of the building with glazed, blank expressions.

They had all heard about the miracle. The paralyzed old woman, already on her deathbed, brought back to life because the boy had touched her. Just once. He had only touched her once. He had walked once in his life, from his bed to the old woman's hut, forcing his twisted limbs to carry him there. To touch the old woman. The few people in the hut had watched the spectacle in amazement. How the old woman stood up afterwards. As if she were a young girl, awakened from a long winter's nap.

Then they had dragged the boy by his twisted limbs back to his parents' town and carried the miracle, the salvation that had appeared to them, out into the world.

Tell us, when will this happen, and what will be the sign of your coming and of the end of the age? Jesus answered: Watch out that no one deceives you. For many will come in my name, claiming, I am the Messiah, and will deceive many. (Matthew 24:3-5)

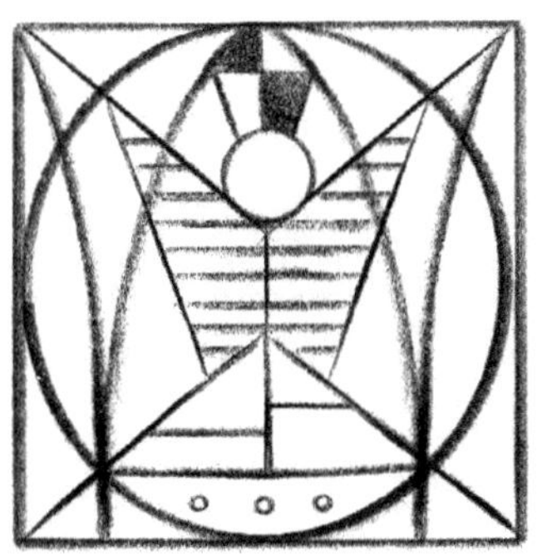

15.

Homeless Foreign homeland

He had arrived barefoot.

He had crossed mountains, forests, streams and roads, injured himself countless times, in the darkness of the night, the only time he could escape. The day was nothing but a large target, prepared for his pursuers. He didn't know if the border was already behind him. You couldn't tell by looking at a tree whether it was native or already foreign. The blades of grass everywhere were just as green, just as free.

Not him. His dark skin color gave him away immediately. Also, the restless look in his eyes. Anyone would read the flight in his face, an open book, just one word, written on two pages, on both sides of life, the past and the future, and in the tiny crack of the book the present: escape.

If anyone still didn't understand, his bare feet would give him away at the latest. Or help. Bare feet. He was in a Christian country. Hadn't the Lord also washed the naked, bruised feet of the others? Good thing he had fled to a Christian country. If he had already crossed the border. It was ten years ago.

He would never forget the image of the first man, a farmer, splendidly dressed, splendidly fed, who set his dog on him, on this thieving pack of gypsies. The first gendarme, correct because the regulations demanded it, otherwise a stony facade of rejection, wall, barbed wire, automatic firing system, trained dogs, minefields, everything was in this facade of a human uniformed being, a thousand times he would rather have fled through a minefield than look into this face.

It had been ten years. Years in asylum homes. Home. What is a home? Alcohol, noisy arguments, threats, theft, no corner of privacy, not for himself alone, certainly not for himself and his wife, but they were still young, in the years of love, in a home, without a place of silence.

They searched for him for ten years. At home. The people he knew. What reaction was in store for him. He had fled. And now returned, a destitute supplicant. There were no more open hands for him. Not in the country he had lived in for ten years, his first roots growing in, his first child born here, not in this home, not in his homeland, a different face, the old homeland unknown, the new one not yet familiar.

Get up, take the child and his mother and go to the land of Israel, for those who were trying to take the child's life are dead.

The war was dead. Died of hunger, because there was nothing left to destroy, nothing left for the war to eat, insatiable as it was.

So he got up, took the child and his mother and went to the land of Israel. But when he heard that Archelaus was reigning in Judea in place of his father Herod, he was afraid to go there. He withdrew to the district of Galilee,...and he went and lived in a town called Nazareth.
(Matthew 2:20-23)

Index

Biography

After graduating from high school in Berlin, I studied
medicine in Berlin and Munich and worked in medicine
for around 40 years after my studies. I have been
retired since the end of 2022. During my professional
career I also wrote some manuscripts, a book for
young people, children's books, novels and poems.
Some have since been self-published.

In addition the author has published several novels in English translation:

Manu's Journey With Death
- A fugue through time

A life, narrated on several levels, accompanied in its tracks and followed by death. In some places, points of this life that have long since passed light up, a brief glowing breath where it pauses for a moment before it is dragged on by the stream of life and disappears somewhere, not without trace but forever. What remains? In any case, death, even if no one is interested in the remnants of this trace of life.

Chrystillian Christmas –
Christmas as usual ~~and~~ different

A goose on its flight to baking-oven land, chasing a golden angel's curl, encountering a mutant Christmas tree, an endless line of waiting stars, Santa's great-great-ancestor and, of course, Father Christmas himself, sitting on a cloud under whose shadow a boy is riding down from the peaks of the Andes, spreading the news of Christ's birth ... It could be like that, but it isn't quite, maybe a little, but just maybe. An Advent calendar of Christmas short stories, profound and loving, varied and multi-faceted, presented in a wonderful narrative style that will enchant even the adult reader. A fragrance-wrapped Christmas soufflé that can be eaten over 26+1 days, on each day of Advent and Christmas plus New Year's Eve, or all at once, depending on the size of your appetite or Christmas taste ...

The Island of Figures
Youth Novel

A little girl in Japan receives a doll from her father for her birthday. When the girl is older, the doll is placed on the waves of the sea in a small boat. Apparently a tradition to mark the transition to a new phase of life into adulthood.

Some time later, another girl travels after her missing doll, and an exciting, adventurous journey begins with an unusual, surprising end.

Allegories
Short Stories Volume 1 -4

The following collection in 4 volumes contains just over 60 short stories, each short story is based on a biblical passage from the New Testament like a parable and is applied to our time. A short time to catch your breath, a short time perhaps to reflect, a short time perhaps to delve deeper. Although Christ used everyday life for his parables, they still leave a deep impression today. They are easy to remember with a hidden important message that we discover when we think about them.

Roxanna
And the Mysterious Monk

Detective Roxanna has solved her first case when life, or rather death, puts another case on her desk. This brings her into contact with a wealthy English gentleman at his country estate, who has amassed a considerable fortune with an unusual business idea. Among them is a complicated hunter, who is not only a little over-the-top in his language, and especially a monk who, with his incredible intuition, not only beats the inspector to it once.

Roxanna
The Fatal Secret of the Murder Books

It begins with a murder, a somewhat bizarre female detective, events that take place in Rome, England and France. A story that jumps back to the Middle Ages, runs on two tracks, two suspicious women and a dead man who suddenly appears one night to one of the two suspects. A tangled criminal string that seems to have been partially untangled by diligent endeavours — only to become even more tangled in the next moment and finally, seemingly lying in front of you untangled in a perfectly straight line.

Uhlenspiegel with the Schilda Citizens

Uhlenspiegel, the lone warrior, armed with an army of mischievous thoughts, encounters a village full of Schilda citizens who are less armed, or rather, armed with different thoughts. Uhlenspiegel's premise: "Where money is at stake, it's good to be good!" And so he mischievously plays out his insights on the Schilda citizens who, with their naive way of thinking, are the appropriate antagonists. Does such an encounter make sense? Amusing and entertaining, in any case!